Stella the Sweet Potato's Amazing Journey

Coloring & Activity Book

Kim David with Stella David

Project Stella Teaching Resource Center

Stella the Sweet Potato's Amazing Journey

Coloring & Activity Book

Kim David with Stella David

Project Stella Teaching Resource Center

Stella the Sweet Potato grew on the ground,

excited to be picked and taken to town.

The truck pulled up, today was the day.

Stella and her friends would be taken away.

Draw a picture of something that makes you feel excited.

She waited patiently, they were coming near.

But what they said filled her eyes with tears.

"You're too big.
You're not pretty.
You have too many spots!
Stay here, under the sun. We'll leave you to rot."

Has something someone said to you made you sad?
Draw a picture of what happened.

Stella was sad as the truck drove down the road.

All of her friends were gone in the load.

Why did this happen?
She did nothing wrong.
But they didn't take her.
She didn't belong.

Then a little later, different trucks arrived...

with people excited for what they would find.

Stella listened with hope to what they would say.

They picked her up and took her away.

"This one is perfect!
She's just what we need.
She has a purpose.
There are many to feed."

Everyone has something they are good at or have a lot of fun doing. Draw a picture of something you enjoy doing or that is your special talent.

She learned there were children with only a little to eat.

Over 16 million in America - that live in need.

The truck went many miles across this great land

and found a group of people lending a helping hand.

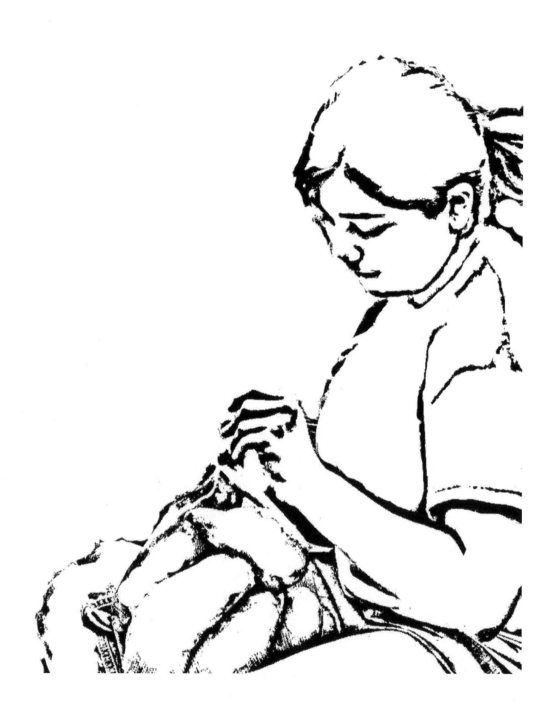

The people gathered together to put to good use

the thousands of potatoes left to the sun's abuse.

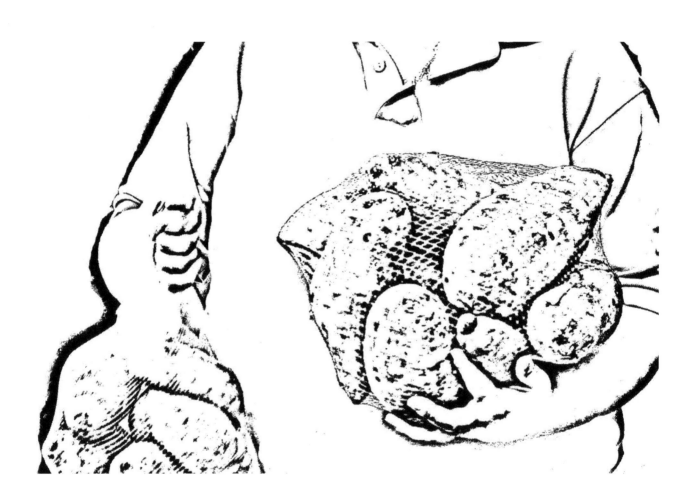

As she was loaded, Stella felt such joy.

She's thankful for her purpose to feed young girls and boys.

Draw a picture of you doing something that helps someone else. How does it make you feel to be helpful?

Thank you to the many volunteers who help provide.

Your purpose is great. Your service can't be denied!

Stella the Sweet Potato's Amazing Journey was first published in 2013 as a children's picture book. The inspiration came when I participated in a Global Youth Service Day Project that April with my (at the time) four year old daughter. It was through a conversation we had about service and volunteerism that the book was developed.

Students at Oxford College of Emory University partnered with community members and the Society of St. Andrew to bag and distribute over 400,000 sweet potatoes through an event called the "Potato Drop". The potatoes were distributed to local churches, food pantries, shelters, and nonprofit organizations committed to feeding individuals and families in need. You can find out more about the Society of St. Andrew by visiting their website at www.endhunger.org.

This was not my first "Potato Drop" and I will forever remember my first event as a student at Georgia College & State University through The G.I.V.E. Center. I grew a lot through the process of seeing the service project come together behind the scenes. I am grateful to The G.I.V.E. Center for all the learning opportunities I experienced with them.

Our hope in writing *Stella the Sweet Potato's Amazing Journey* is that a new generation of service-minded youth will discover volunteerism and that each person has the very special ability to make a difference.

These next pages include additional

activity pages for you to enjoy!

What can you make with Sweet Potatoes?

Stella the Sweet Potato's Word Search

T	Y	L	L	I	H	A	S	H	H	O	E
U	C	O	M	A	S	H	E	D	C	E	T
O	A	K	M	I	T	I	O	N	P	L	H
S	S	H	O	S	M	U	P	G	E	I	U
T	S	S	F	I	O	O	A	S	U	N	E
A	E	E	A	L	V	U	S	I	B	L	E
N	R	H	V	A	C	A	P	I	A	N	I
E	O	O	F	Z	V	I	E	A	K	I	R
M	L	S	R	E	R	L	B	N	E	G	S
J	E	P	I	E	A	S	A	R	D	H	S
B	T	C	E	N	F	I	K	E	N	T	T
H	O	P	S	O	S	I	E	I	O	N	E
S	H	A	E	T	W	E	D	E	L	P	L
O	T	R	O	A	S	T	E	D	A	T	O

Baked   Casserole

Fries   Hash

Mashed   Pie

Roasted   Soup

CELEBRATE WHAT MAKES YOU DIFFERENT!

Circle the differences you find between the two Stella the Sweet Potato characters.

Help Stella the Sweet Potato make it through the maze and get loaded onto the truck.

Volunteering with other people is a lot of fun and can also make a difference in your community.

Unscramble the words below to see who you can volunteer with.

N R E F I D S	
Y M A L F I	
O C S U T S	
H R C U C H	
O L C S O H	

Design your own Stella the Sweet Potato!

It is okay to feel many different emotions – just like Stella the Sweet Potato feels throughout the story. Draw your own characters below to show different feelings – HAPPY, SAD, EXCITED, and MAD

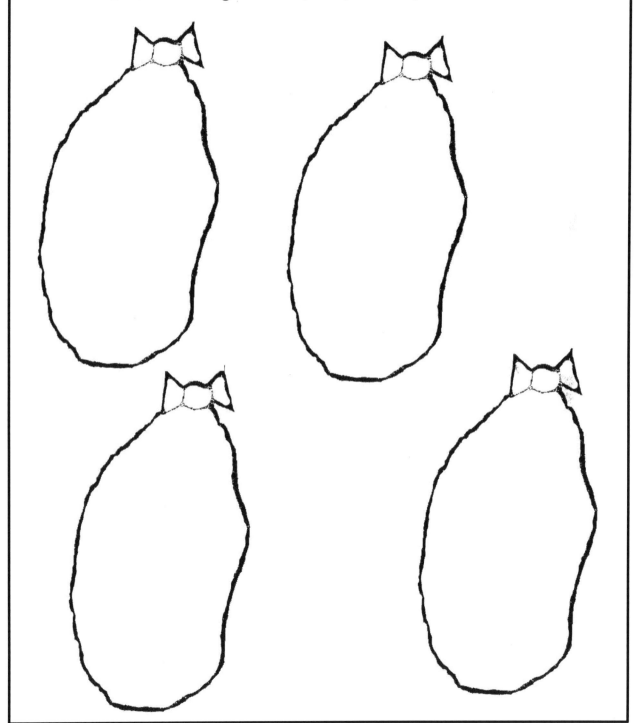

Create your Own Characters!

These are just some of the fruits and vegetables that can be gleaned and used to help feed people that are hungry.

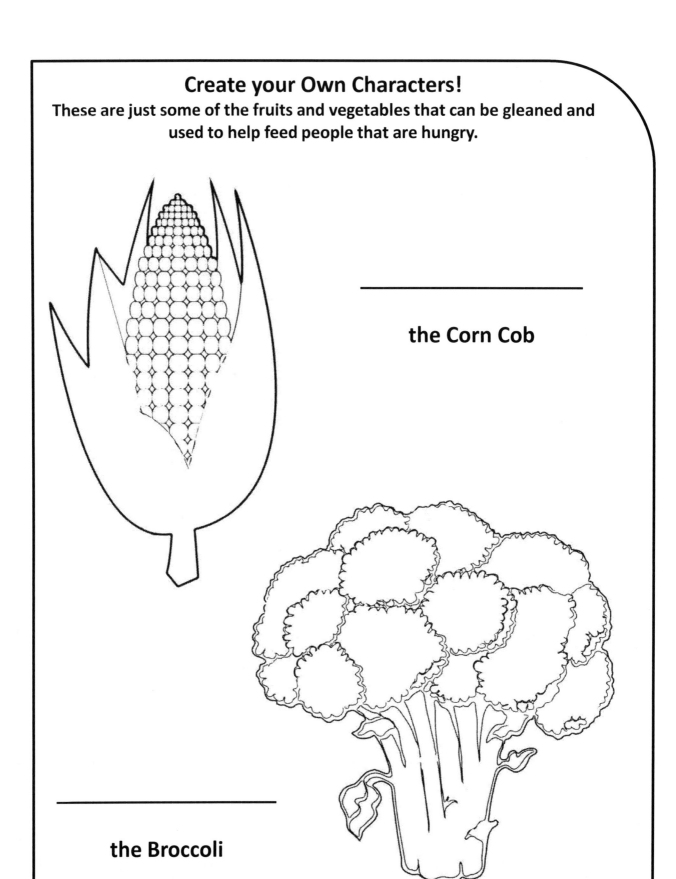

the Corn Cob

the Broccoli

Don't forget to give each character a name!

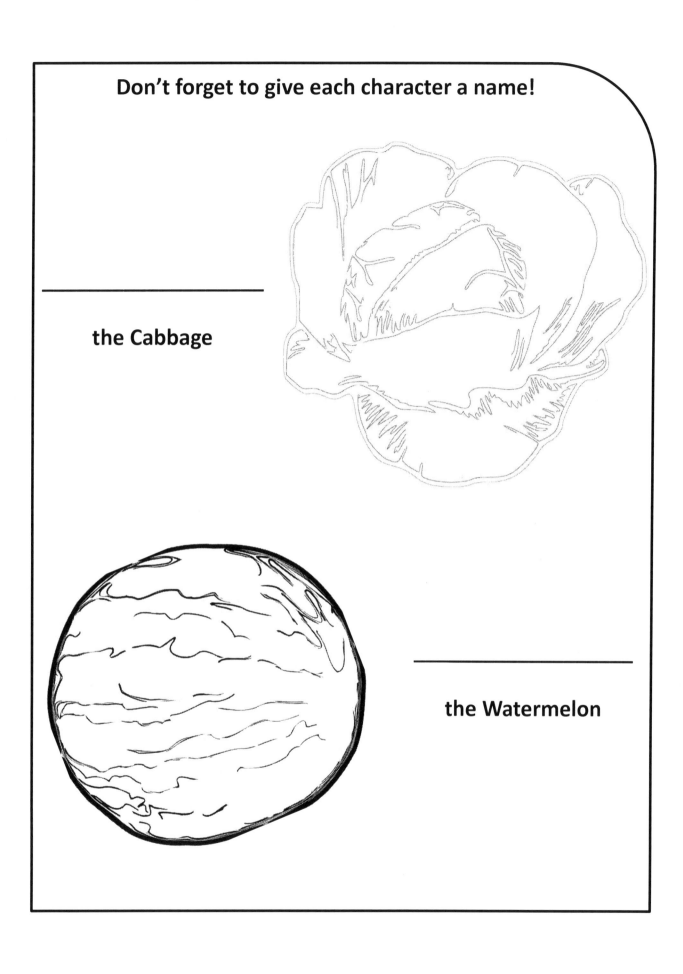

_____

the Cabbage

_____

the Watermelon

Project Stella Teaching Resource Center was founded by Kim David while pursuing her Master of Library and Information Science degree at Wayne State University. The mission of Project Stella TRC is to provide hands on educational resources for teachers, families and community groups.

Kim David can be contacted by email at projectstellatrc@gmail.com or through Facebook @projectstellaTRC.

Other books include:

Journey of Faith Into the Desert: A Nine Week Devotional Journal

How Do You Spell Missions?

*Service Project Coordinator Workbook: Starting with the Basics
(Project Stella TRC Service-based Curriculum)*

Acts of Compassion: An Alternative Break Challenge: Journal for Students

Made in the USA
Columbia, SC
07 March 2025